First there was grass, then flowers, then trees, then animals, and last men and women; and this is how it came to be.

MOON MOTHER

A NATIVE AMERICAN CREATION TALE

Adapted and illustrated by

ED YOUNG

WILLA PERLMAN BOOKS
AN IMPRINT OF HARPERCOLLINS PUBLISHERS

THE EARTH was very beautiful; there was no cold; it was summer always. Grass, flowers, and trees covered the face of the earth; there were lakes and rivers.

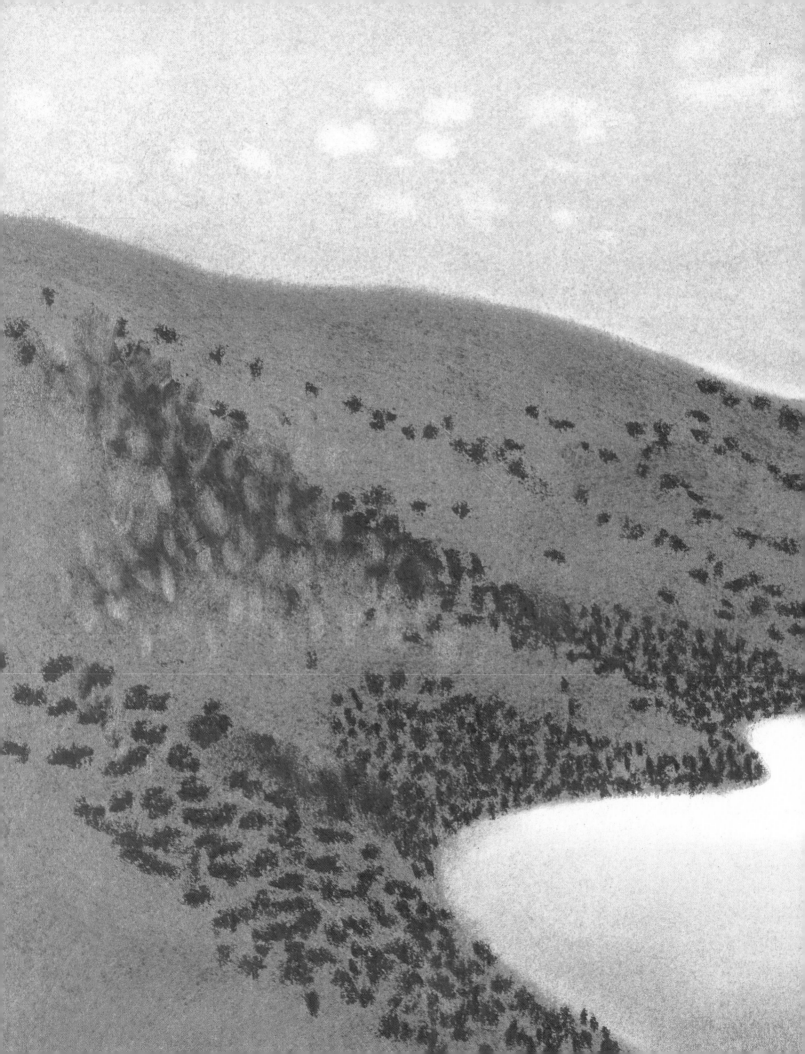

There were nuts, fruits, roots, and berries, but there was no one to eat them. Then a spirit person saw this beautiful place and said, "I will live here." But soon he became very lonesome, so he amused himself by making the animals.

He made the fishes and taught them to swim.
He made the birds and taught them to fly.

He made the foxes, coyotes, bears, raccoons, squirrels, deer, and all animals, and taught them how to live.

After a time he tired of his creatures and of making new animals. He longed for some friends and companions.

Therefore he made images of himself, and warmed them and made them alive; and this is how men came to be.

He talked with the men and taught them how to make spears, bows, arrows, and knives. He showed them how to weave blankets, build houses, make fire, and how to roast their food and burn clay to make pots.

Then the animals complained to the spirit person that his new creatures hunted and slew them, so to each he gave some protection against the men. The skunk had been his pet and was very tame, so to him he gave the surest safeguard of all.

In this manner the spirit person and the men lived very happily for a long time; but after a time there came out of the sky another spirit person, a woman, and she lived near a lake in a beautiful valley. It was not very long until the first spirit person found the woman spirit person, and, because she was of his own kind, he remained with her.

Then the men went to him and said, "Have you forgotten us?" But he said, "Do as I have taught you, and the earth will care for you."

But the men began to quarrel and fight among themselves. Finally, one man by his bravery, strength, and quickness became chief among the men; and he said, "Come, let us go to our good friend." So they went together to the house of the spirit people, but they had gone away, and in the silence the men were awestruck and dared not go farther.

The chief went forward, when there came a wail from inside the sacred house that chilled their blood, and great fear seized their hearts.

The chief was courageous, as a chief ought to be. He went to the sacred house, and there upon the threshold lay a newborn girl baby. The spirit people had gone, but they had left a gift for the men.

And when the night came, there was a new light in the sky, and the men saw that the moon was the face of the woman spirit person, who is carried across the sky every night by her husband, that she may play with the stars. The chief took the baby to his house, and all the men waited upon her.

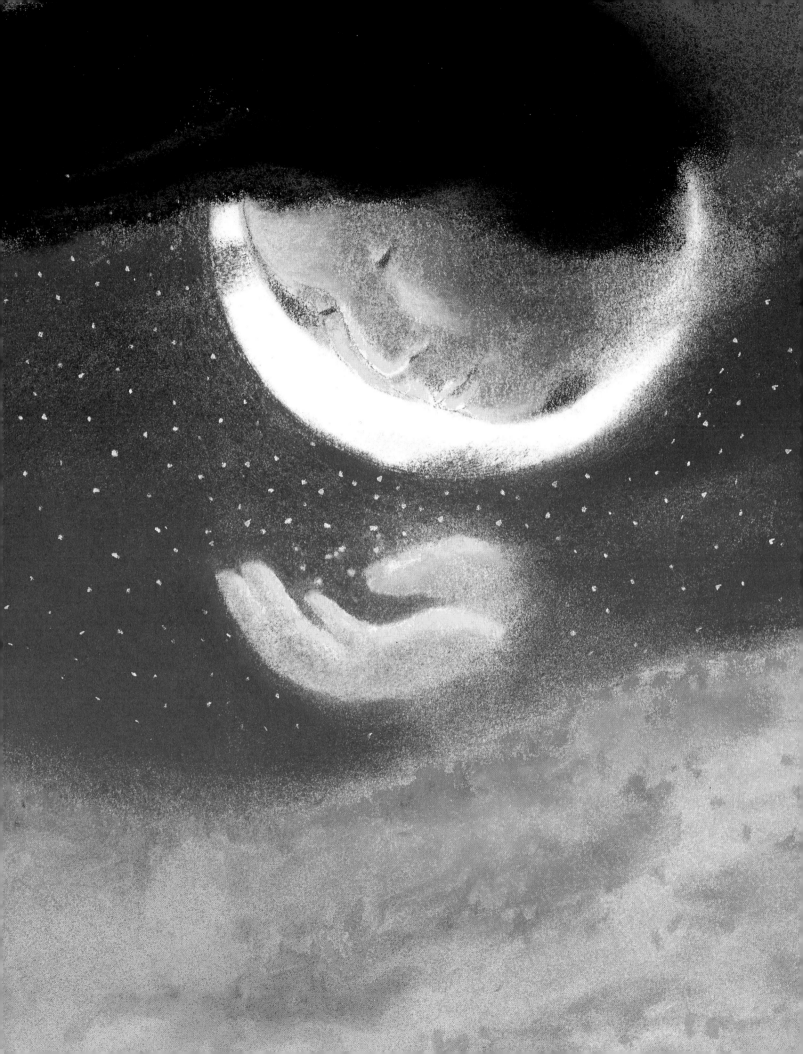

She was changeful as the moon, and in time
she became a woman. Then the chief took her as
his wife and from these two came all people.

And now when a baby is born, he cries,
because he has left the moon-land and has lost
his moon mother.

And when one is old and feeble, he dies when
the moon mother's face is turned away from him.

The display type for MOON MOTHER: *A Native American Creation Tale* was set in Amsterdam Studio Light.
The text was composed in Garamond No. 3 Bold.
The paintings were executed in pastel on 100% rag paper.
The transparencies were made by Studio Chrome, New York, New York.
The color separations were made by Vimnice Printing Press Co., Ltd., Hong Kong.
The entire book was printed by Berryville Graphics, Berryville, Virginia, on Patina Matte
    made by Lindenmeyr Book Publishing Papers, New York, New York.
Bound by Berryville Graphics, Berryville, Virginia.
Production supervision by Lucille Schneider and John Vitale.
Designed by Ed Young and Christine Kettner.

Moon Mother: A Native American Creation Tale is adapted from a story called "How Animals and People Were Made,
and How the Moon was Placed in the Sky" retold by Charles Erskine Scott Wood, first published in 1901 as part of a
collection titled *A Book of Tales: Being Some Myths of the North American Indians.*

Moon Mother
A Native American Creation Tale
Copyright © 1993 by Ed Young.   Printed in the U.S.A.   All rights reserved.
1 2 3 4 5 6 7 8 9 10 ❖ First Edition

Library of Congress Cataloging-in-Publication Data
Young, Ed.
   Moon mother : a Native American creation tale / adapted and illustrated by Ed Young.
      p.   cm.
   "Willa Perlman books."
   Summary: A retelling of a traditional Native American tale in which a spirit person that made animals and
people falls in love with a woman spirit person who becomes the moon he carries through the sky every night.
      ISBN 0-06-021301-9. — ISBN 0-06-021302-7 (lib. bdg.)
   1. Indians of North America—Legends. [1. Indians of North America—Legends.]   I. Young, Ed, ill.   II. Title.
E98.F6W825   1993   92-14981
398.2'08997—dc20   CIP
                                                                                                            AC

With gratitude to Chieh Chieh,
a guardian angel in disguise for
me and everyone in the family
—E. Y.